Contents

HOWARDS WHO'S WHO

Here is Howard.
He likes
roller skating,
watching TV
and doing
difficult jigsaws.
Favourite smell:
fried onions.
Favourite taste:
peanut butter.

This is Howard's
sister, Alice.
She collects things -
pebbles,
china ornaments
and Anything Pink.
She plays tennis
and basketball,
(but not at
the same time).

HOORAY FOR HOWARD

Stories and Pictures by Colin West

Young Lions
An Imprint of HarperCollinsPublishers

First published in Great Britain 1993 in Young Lions
3 5 7 9 10 8 6 4 2

Young Lions is an imprint of
the Children's Division, part of
HarperCollins Publishers Ltd,
77–85 Fulham Palace Road,
Hammersmith, London W6 8JB

ISBN 0 00 674470 2

Printed and bound in Great Britain by
HarperCollins Manufacturing, Glasgow

Howard's mum and dad have been married for as long as anyone can remember.

His mum likes tinkering with cars and watching keep-fit videos.
His dad is a keen gardener and a D.I.Y. enthusiast. He works in a bank.

So that's Howard's family, now let's hear about his friends...

Ronald is Howard's
best friend.
He likes wearing
fancy clothes.
He also enjoys
waterski-ing and
black and white
Tarzan movies.
He wants to be
a famous writer.

Lucy is
Howard's
special friend.
She's a tapir.
She likes pop
music,
dancing and
weight training.
She likes
Howard a lot.

Englebert lives
next door to Howard.
He's only little
and likes playing
around.
He sometimes rides
his scooter
on the pavement.

Now you've heard about Howard's
family and friends, you can read
some stories about them all....

HOWARD HURTS HIS TOE

One day Howard had an accident.
He tripped over a loose roller skate
and stubbed his toe.
It really hurt.
His mother looked at his sore toe.

"You won't be able to run around for a while," she warned him. "Serves you right for not putting away your things!" added his sister Alice.

Howard sat by himself.
He could hear laughter
coming from outside.

Howard stood up and hobbled
around. His toe was painful, but he
managed to limp outside.
His little neighbour Englebert was
kicking a ball against the wall.
"Hello Howard!" he called. "Come
and join me in a game of football."

"I'd love to," explained Howard, "but
I've stubbed my toe and
I can only hobble."
"What a shame," said Englebert.

A little way down the road,
Howard saw his friend Lucy who
was running along flying a kite.
"Hi, Howard, come and take hold of
the string for a while!" she cried.
"I'd love to, but I've stubbed my toe,
and I can only hobble," explained
Howard.
"Oh, I'm sorry," said Lucy.
Just then his friend Ronald passed by.
"Hey, Howard, I'm going for a row
down the river - come and join me!"
he said.

"I'd love to," said Howard, "but I've stubbed my toe and I can only hobble."

"Don't worry," replied Ronald. "I'll give you a piggyback ride."

Howard agreed, and climbed on Ronald's back.

Ronald was glad to get to the boathouse at last.

Howard hopped off.

Ronald paid for a boat, and helped Howard aboard.

Ronald was good at rowing,
and Howard sat back
and enjoyed the view.

"Wow! Look at that butterfly!"
Howard said excitedly.
A little further down river, Ronald
pointed out some big fish
through the clear water.

Then they saw a handsome kingfisher.
"Wow! I've never seen one before!"
said Howard.

The afternoon was full of other
surprises too:

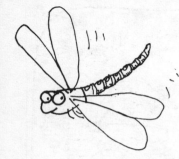 a beautiful dragonfly,

a green and
yellow frog,

 and a bird's nest
full of eggs.

When it was getting late, and
Ronald's arms were beginning
to ache, he rowed back to
the boathouse.

"I've had a great time today!" said
Howard as he got out.
"Good," said Ronald. "I hope your
toe is better tomorrow."
"My toe?" said Howard. "Hey!
I'd forgotten I'd ever stubbed it!"
And Howard wasn't hobbling
any more.

HOWARD'S PRESENT

Howard's special friend Lucy
had a birthday the next day.
Howard counted his pocket money.
He had two pounds and forty-three
pence. He wanted to buy Lucy
something nice.
But he couldn't think what.

Howard went to the shops
to get some ideas.
He passed a clothes shop.
In the window were some
lovely dresses and things.
But they all cost more than
two pounds forty-three.

Howard went into the record shop
next door.
But they didn't have any records
by Lucy's favourite group,
The Wailing Warthogs.

Next was the hardware store
on the corner.
They had plenty of candles
and boot polish.
They weren't too expensive.
But Howard didn't think candles
and boot polish would make
a very good present.

Over the road was
"Carlo's Candy Store".
"This could be the answer,"
thought Howard.
He went in to see what Carlo had.

Howard bought the biggest box
of chocolates he could get for
two pounds forty-three.

Howard went home singing.
He took the chocolates to his room.
"Lucy will love them," he thought.

He put the box on his bedside table.
He could hardly wait for Lucy's
birthday tomorrow.

That night Howard had a strange
dream. He dreamed he gave Lucy
her birthday present.
When she opened the box, it was
full of candles and boot polish.

Howard woke up with a start.
He was worried his box of
chocolates had turned into
candles and boot polish.
Howard put on the light.

It still *looked* like a box of chocolates.
But he had to be certain.
So he opened the lid and
peeked inside.
Howard breathed a sigh of relief.
There were chocolates inside after all.
But supposing the chocolates had
candle and boot polish centres?

Howard had to be certain.
So he nibbled one of the chocolates.
It was strawberry cream.
But supposing one of the others...?

To make certain, Howard nibbled
some more. Soon he had eaten the
lot. Not one of them tasted of
candles or boot polish.

Howard smiled to himself
and went back to sleep.

When Howard next woke up,
it was eight o'clock in the morning.
He had tummy ache.

"Oh no, I've eaten Lucy's birthday present," Howard sighed. Just then his mum popped her head round the door.

"Hurry up, Howard," she said. "Lucy has called to show you one of her birthday presents."

Howard got dressed and went
downstairs to face Lucy.
He wondered what he could
say to her.

Lucy was waiting outside.
"Happy birthday..." Howard began.
"Thanks Howard," replied Lucy.
"Just look at my new bicycle."

"Wow!" said Howard. "I like
the silver mudguards."
Then he thought he should explain
about his own present.

"I bought you some nice chocolates,"
he said, "but I ate them all to make
sure they weren't made of candles
or boot polish."
"I see," said Lucy. She thought
it was an odd excuse.
"Are you feeling all right?"
she asked.
"I've got a bit of a tummy ache,"
confessed Howard.

"I'm not surprised," said Lucy.
"But would you like to go for
a bike ride anyway?"
"OK," said Howard.

Howard got his bike from the shed.
Lucy and Howard rode three times
round the block.

Lucy told Howard it really didn't
matter about the chocolates.
"I'm trying to lose weight, anyway,"
she said.
"I like you the way you are,"
said Howard.

Lucy blushed bright pink.
Howard said the sweetest things!

HOWARD UP A TREE

One day Howard noticed a tent in
his neighbour's back garden.
Before long Englebert popped out
his head.

"Look at me, I've set up camp!"
said Englebert.
"I can see that," said Howard.
"Can you teach me to be a scout?"
asked Englebert.
"Of course I can!" said Howard.

Howard climbed over the fence.
He could teach Englebert all
he knew about scouting.

"To be a good scout, you need to be a good look-out," said Howard. "So you have to learn to climb trees."

Howard looked at the trees in Englebert's garden.
"Let's start with that one," he said.
Howard pointed to a tree by the fence.
"It's very big," said Englebert.
Howard started climbing up.

Howard soon reached the first branch.
"I'm already as high as the tent!"
he cried.
He climbed up further.

Howard got to the next branch.
"Now I can see over the roof tops
to the river and the boathouse!"
"Mind how you go!" shouted Englebert.

Howard went one branch up.
But he had a shock when he looked
down. Englebert looked really tiny
standing below.

There was still a way to go
if Howard wanted to show how
to be a good look-out.

Howard went to the next branch,
but he began to feel dizzy.
"Are you all right?" cried Englebert.
Howard couldn't speak.
The branch creaked.
Howard was scared to move.

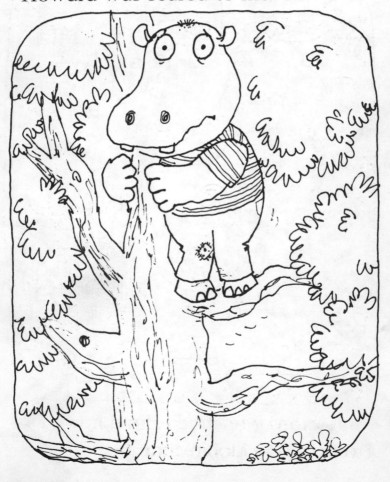

Englebert wondered how he could
help. In the end he went indoors to
find his mum. She was feeding Sam,
their pet goldfish.
"Howard is stuck up a tree,"
Englebert explained.

Mrs Alligator fetched a ladder.
She leaned it against the tree.

Then Mrs Alligator climbed up
until she reached Howard.
She put him over her shoulder
and clambered down.

Howard sat in a chair until
he felt better.
Englebert brought him some cocoa.
It was a long while before Howard
gave Englebert any more lessons
in climbing trees.

HOWARD AND THE LAST PEACH

There was just one peach left
in the fruit bowl.
Howard really wanted it.
But he knew it would be wrong
to take it without asking
if anyone else would like it.

Howard found his mother.
She was fixing the car.
"Mum, do you mind if I have
the last peach?" he asked.
"I don't mind, Howard, but ask
your father first in case he'd like it,"
his mother replied.

Howard found his father.
He was putting up some pictures.
"Dad, do you mind if I have
the last peach?" he asked.

"I don't mind," his father replied,
"but ask Alice first in case
she'd like it."
"OK, Dad," said Howard.

But Howard was worried now.
He knew his sister Alice would never
agree to let him have the last peach.
She'd say she wanted it,
even if she didn't,
just to stop Howard from having it.
What was he to do?

Howard went to his room and put
up his DO NOT DISTURB sign.
Then he sat down at his desk
and thought good and hard.
He thought for over half an hour
until he had an idea.

Now... maybe Howard could tell
Alice he *didn't* want the last peach.
Then she would say: "Neither do I."
Then he'd say suddenly:
"I've changed my mind!"
Then before she could say anything,
he could take it fair and square.
Howard chuckled to himself.
It was the perfect plan.

He went to find his sister.

Alice was reading downstairs.
"Hey, Alice," he said, "you know
that last peach, well, I don't want it,
you know."
"Is that so?" said Alice,
and she went back to her book.

"I'll have to repeat the message,"
thought Howard.
He cleared his throat.
"Hey, Alice," he said, "I just *couldn't*
eat that last peach, you know."
"I know you couldn't," said Alice,
"because I've already had it!"

Howard was really mad.
"You never asked me if I wanted it!"
he protested.
"I tried to," replied Alice, "but when I
went to ask you, you'd put up your
DO NOT DISTURB sign, so I just had
to go ahead. It's just as well you
didn't want it."

"Humph!" said Howard, and he
stormed out.

"What a crafty sister I've got,"
said Howard.
"I did all that hard thinking
for nothing!"